PRAISE FOR
THE CURIOUS GIRAFFE

Des Hague, 9XCEO, and Co-Founder of Nebula9 Spirits

The Curious Giraffe is a masterclass that illustrates the issues of today's education system through powerful, clever and unique storytelling. The fact that the narrative is also written by a nine-year-old is simply amazing. This book is a must read.

Paul L Gunn Jr., CEO KUOG Corporation and Bestselling Author

Standing tall and the divergence of thought with action to cement its intangible wealth is meaningful for what legacy impact can come from it. Curiosity has its benefits in life for discovery and wonder found. It is often prominent in those successful entrepreneurs as well across those in many domains to aid in value contributions to this world. The perpetual benefits of gaining knowledge for applied wisdom weights. Hindering the intensity of curiosity as well as foregoing its cultivation in our youth may lessen the ability for true education to take place in the confines of the walls of youth as sequestered too. Zoraib brings a meaningful illustration of a heroic giraffe to champion in relation to what many youth are enduring who seek to further their knowledge. This is a wonderful story that youth and adults can find relation to their own lives and applaud the Giraffe for securing what is needed to elevate. This is a heartwarming and meaningful read for all to enjoy. I was personally touched by Zoraib's keen sense to share in a manner from being anchored in wisdom of the heart and a radiance to uplift those who read.

Bret Packard, Founder, Bret Packard Enterprises
Embracing passion and curiosity transforms learning into an enjoyable experience, inspiring and unlocking the benefits of critical thinking. By doing so, individuals can surpass the limits imposed by conventional methods.

Lameen Abdul Malik
Nobel Peace Prize Winner and CEO of Honest Management
A famous scholar once cautioned us to not teach our children in the manner that we were taught

because there was a generational gap and it may be akin to solving today's problems with yesterday's solutions. So, on reading through this book, I was pleased to see that not only had a young (9 year old) boy already frustrated with the current educational system, seized the initiative to voice out his opinions about it, but to creatively communicate his frustration in a beautiful story depicting characters that his age groups and others much older than him can relate to, with a quest not just to learn differently but also to serve humanity. Brilliant indeed.

Michael Pederson
Author of Atomic Actions

I have always felt the education system is greatly flawed and needs a new direction. Giraffe's quest in the Amazon is a captivating tale that brilliantly reimagines education through adventure and discovery. The story's fusion of courage, empathy, and self-discovery against the backdrop of the mythical El Dorado is both inspiring and thought-provoking. An essential read for anyone passionate about transforming traditional learning into an exciting, experiential journey.

Preston Weekes, Co-Founder of the Save Lives Project

The Story of Giraffe is mirror to the way many children feel today as the worlds education system rapidly transforms to our modern world.

THE CURIOUS GIRAFFE

A Jungle Discovery of the Truth

BY Zoraib Nadeem

First edition published by 10 Step Books

Prepared for publication and cover design by 10 Step Books

Editing and layout by Lupi Docs & Designs/Rich Pageant Media

ISBN: 978-1-7339561-7-8 (paperback)
ISBN: 978-1-7339561-8-5 (ebook)

DEDICATION

This book is dedicated with profound gratitude to my mother, Ambreen Nadeem, whose unwavering support made it possible for me to complete this work. Her understanding of my unconventional approach to learning has empowered me to my transform ideas into this book.

To my father, Nadeem Shahzad, whose encouragement and support have been my guiding light throughout every step of this transformative journey.

To my siblings, Aheed Nadeem and Zuha Nadeem, whose support and collaboration have been invaluable, helping me moving forward whenever I was stuck with the storyline.

And, last but certainly not least, this dedication extends to everyone with a desire to explore learning in their own unique way. May this book inspire and resonate with your individual journey of discovery.

TABLE OF CONTENTS

CHAPTER ONE

THE USUAL ARGUMENT

"Wake up! Wake up! It's school time." His Mom shouted.

Giraffe half-opened his eyes and saw the time, the clock showed 6 o'clock in the morning. He closed his eyes again and thought, "Oh no, not again." He said to his Mom. "I do not want to go to school." His Mom replied, "It is out of the question. You have to go to school."

Giraffe said, "Why exactly? Around 90-95% of what I learn in school won't ever be used again. That is approximately fifteen or seventeen years of our lives wasted."

His Mom replied, "Every job requires a certain degree. If you do not study you will not be able to get a decent job and have a good life."

Giraffe responded "Why do I need a job? Can't I learn to survive in the wilderness?"

His Mom said, "We are not super rich, who can survive without finding a job? Your father is earning money because he is employed at a good company and that is how he fulfills our needs. He pays our bills because he earns money through his job. How will you pay your bills, if you do not study now?"

Giraffe said, "We do not need degrees to make money, we can read books or make a small business. There are many successful people who don't have a degree, Mother. For example, Steve Jobs was the co-founder of Apple and one of the most successful entrepreneurs of our time. He dropped out of Reed College after one semester. Mark Zuckerberg is the founder and CEO of Facebook. He did not complete his degree. And oh, Richard Branson...Richard Branson is the founder of the Virgin Group. He dropped out of school at the age of 16. Cristiano Ronaldo's worth is $500 million and he has not even received his schooling, as he got expelled at the age of 14 so be honest with me, why do we need a degree?"

His Mom replied, "I agree that all those people made their fortune without any degree. But there are only a handful of people who made it to the top without a degree. Not everyone can reach that level without a degree. Common people need a degree to get a decent job."

Giraffe clicked his tongue and said, "Mama, don't you want me to be an uncommon and successful person?"

She looked at her beloved son still refusing to get out of bed and said, "Honey, I want you to be very very successful. And I know that you need to go to school now. No more arguments, get up!"

Giraffe said "The only time I will go to school is when you satisfy my questions. You just showed me that you don't have an answer for that.

His Mother replied "Son please don't be a pain, and go to school, I know what's best for you."

Giraffe thought to himself, "Well, maybe I should just go to school. I do have three friends and Mom is very strict, so maybe today will be a good day, and I will enjoy it."

* * * * *

Giraffe's family is a loving and unique one. His mother, a dedicated housewife, is the heart of their home. She takes care of their house and family with unwavering love and commitment, especially toward her son, Giraffe. His father, on the other hand, works diligently as an administrator in a company. He is a hardworking and loving dad, but his job often keeps him at work late into the evening, a sacrifice he makes to provide for his family.

Giraffe himself is a remarkable individual among giraffes. He possesses an insatiable curiosity and a deep-seated disdain for the rigid (and in his opinion, outdated) education system. He firmly believes that genuine learning occurs outside the confines of traditional classrooms and textbooks. His unquenchable thirst for knowledge leads him on extraordinary adventures, seeking to discover the world's wonders firsthand.

Giraffe lives with his family in Costa Rica, in a medium-sized house from inside a small jungle. He always wanted to go to the Amazon Rainforest mum and dad are very strict. He does not have a brother or sister, he's always very hyperactive and curious to find out more about different things in life. He doesn't like the ways the teachers teach in the school; he feels like there are much more efficient ways teachers can teach, and he always seems to outsmart a teacher in a question that he actually could use in life.

Another day started at school, and Giraffe already began to feel bored. In the confines of the classroom, he started feeling suffocated. Where the air was stifled with the repetition of stale lectures, Giraffe found himself wrestling with the constraints of monotony. The familiar teacher's voice, regurgitating lessons for what felt like the umpteenth time, gnawed at his spirit. Restless and yearning for more, he longed to escape the classroom, where time trickled by at an agonizing pace. With every tick of the clock, his imagination soared beyond the confines of the four walls, beckoning him to seek the thrill of a more stimulating and purposeful pursuit.

The lecture went on, and he felt like he was in a state of limbo. He slipped into the imagination of gaming to seek thrill in that boring lecture. He embarked on a thrilling odyssey through the vivid landscapes of his Blox video game, assuming an avatar voraciously devouring fruits to amass untold power, and unlocking gateways to uncharted realms.

Lost in the feeling of relaxation and playing games, he continued to explore his thoughts on the new release of Blox, which happened today, but the school day gave him no time to enjoy it. He started playing the game in his mind and gaining more power to access different islands. In his imagination, he kept eating fruits, exploring the unknown, and seeking adventures.

As he drifted through the Blox world, the teacher's discerning gaze caught his lack of focus during the lecture. "Giraffe," she called, startling him. "Can you tell me which planet is the farthest one?"

Caught off guard, he felt a flicker of confusion, his attention having strayed from the lesson. Gathering his wits, he recalled a YouTube video that had delved into the intricacies of the topic. With confidence, he replied, "Kepler 22b is the farthest earth-like planet, situated 587 light years away from Earth. And you know what, it's strikingly similar to our own planet."

A small smile crept onto his face as he knew he had given the correct answer. Yet, the teacher's reaction was not what he expected. She continued to regard him with a peculiar expression before letting out a chuckle. "What is Kepler 22b? I was only inquiring about the farthest planet in our solar system. Your mind was wandering, lost in your imagination."

Giraffe couldn't help but interject, "But teacher, I provided additional information."

In response, the teacher gently remarked, "Your knowledge might have been more extensive, but it wasn't necessary."

Disheartened, Giraffe couldn't shake off the disappointment that settled within him.

He wants to experience different aspects of life away from school. Giraffe knows he could learn amazing things if he could only visit the Amazon Rainforest. He often begs his Mom to go to the Amazon, but his Mom always says no. His Mom would say, "Why do you want to go to the Amazon? It is a very dangerous forest, full of snakes and dangerous animals. One type of snake is the Anaconda, they are bigger than giraffes, and can swallow whole animals. The weather also is so unpredictable that you would never know what to expect. There could be sudden storms and flooding."

The more his Mom talked about the dangers of the Amazon Rainforest, the more he was fascinated by it. Giraffe imagined walking among the amazing plants and learning about how they grow in different habitats. He then thought about all the different animal species that could live there.

Once his mom told him about El Dorado, a city of Gold that legend says is buried in the Amazon Rainforest. She told him the story that long ago; El Dorado was a very rich city. Everything in that city was made of Gold. In order to protect their wealth, people of their city, used to cover themselves in gold dust and then rolled in Lake Guatavita to offer their riches to the ancient figures who protected the city, but once the king did not offer the gold to the ancient figures, so they got angry with the king. The ancient figures cursed the city and buried it below the rainforest. Since then, many people have gone to Amazon in search of the lost city of Gold, but no one has found it yet.

Giraffe was so fascinated by the story and wanted to see the city with his own eyes. He often used to imagine walking in the city made of Gold and he dreamed of finding the city.

CHAPTER TWO

MISUNDERSTOOD

The usual day at school started. He forced himself to go to school. As he stepped inside, the room filled with the chattering of his classmates. Sam, the monkey, swung down from a vine and landed next to Giraffe, excitement lighting up his expressive eyes. "Hey, Giraffe, did you hear about the mangoes in the east clearing? They're supposed to be huge this season!"

Giraffe nodded with a faint smile, "Yes, I did. The weather patterns seem to have favored them this year." Just then, Toucan hopped in, flapping his wings and settling on a branch nearby. "Have you two heard about the game of camouflage we played yesterday? It was amazing! We need to do it again."

Alex, the curious anteater, joined the conversation. He asked about the upcoming test on the Solar

System. Giraffe, feeling a surge of enthusiasm, started discussing the complexities of the planetary orbits and the fascinating details about each celestial body. "Did you know that Jupiter is so massive that it could fit all the other planets within it? And Saturn's rings are made of ice particles and rock dust!"

However, his excitement was met with snickers and chuckles from the others. "Oh, here goes Giraffe, the know-it-all nerd," one of them jeered, while another rolled their eyes and whispered, "He's always talking about things no one cares about. What a bore!" Sam said.

Toucan added, "Giraffe, you're always going on about these weird things no one understands. Stick to something we actually care about," one of them remarked, shaking his head.

Giraffe's heart sank, and he lowered his head, trying to hide the hurt. Despite his efforts to fit in, he couldn't shake the feeling of being an outcast. As the class continued to giggle and whisper among themselves, he made a silent promise to himself to keep pursuing his passion for knowledge, no matter what others thought of him.

The teacher arrived in the class and the science test began. Giraffe moved through the questions with ease, and was quite proud of his responses which included some additional information.

The next day, the teacher stood at the front of the classroom, a pile of graded papers in hand. Giraffe's heart raced with anticipation as the teacher began to announce the results. Sam and Toucan leaned in, eager to hear how they had fared.

"Sam, excellent work. Keep it up," the teacher praised, handing back his paper with a big red star. Toucan received similar words of encouragement for his efforts. Giraffe's hooves tapped nervously on the wooden floor as the teacher approached him. The teacher's expression was inscrutable as she handed over the graded paper.

Giraffe hesitated for a moment before looking closely at the paper, his heart sinking as he scanned the marks. Despite feeling confident about the test, it seemed the teacher didn't agree with his remarkable answers. His brow furrowed, and he felt himself starting to sweat a little bit, trying to comprehend the low score.

Sam asked, "What grade did you get on the Science test? "

Giraffe replied sheepishly, "Oh I failed," the boys laughed at him.

Alex said, "Hah! You're so dumb, I got a way better grade than you."

Toucan joined the chastising, "I know, right? It was soo easy I could have slept through it."

Mark, at last said, "That test was so easy it was pretty much impossible to fail, I can't believe you failed it! What, did you fall asleep studying?"

The rest of the day for Giraffe was a nightmare from which he couldn't wait to wake up. He crawled into bed as soon as he was finished with his dinner, just wanting to make the day go away. His mother was worried he might be sick, but decided to let her growing boy sleep. Afterall, it did give her extra time to relax without Giraffe's endless questions and complaints about having to go to school.

The next morning, Giraffe woke up and said to himself "Hmm, maybe I should work harder, maybe I should study more and try to pass the exams."

In simple words he tried to be very positive; he did want his Mom and Dad to be proud of him.

He jumped out of bed with enthusiasm and positivity. He began his day in a happy mood, determined to have a better day. After brushing his hair and teeth, he dressed in his favorite jungle print shirt, and went downstairs humming his favorite song, "*Touch the Sky*" by Julie Fowlis.

> *I will ride, I will fly*
> *Chase the wind and touch the sky*
> *I will fly*
> *Chase the wind and touch the sky*
>
> *Where dark woods hide secrets*
> *And mountains are fierce and bold*
> *Deep waters hold reflections*
> *Of times lost long ago*
>
> *I will hear their every story*
> *Take hold of my own dream*
> *Be as strong as the seas are stormy*
> *And proud as an eagle's scream*

He sat at the family table for breakfast, and saw his mum and dad preparing almond cake for him, which was not his favorite, but he just ate it for the sake of his parent's happiness. He was positive and was grateful.

On the school bus, frustration gnawed at Giraffe. Upon arriving at school, his classmate, Alex the Monkey, approached him. "Hey, what level did you reach in Blox?" Alex inquired.

With excitement, Giraffe responded, "I'm at level 1487. How about you?"

Alex shrugged, admitting, "I'm only at level 415. How do you manage to reach such high levels?"

Giraffe explained, "I grind a lot."

"But isn't it boring?" Alex questioned.

Giraffe replied, "It's a sacrifice worth making. Patience helps you reach higher levels. But if it's not your thing, you can play something else. I know some cool zombie games."

After the discussion about his favorite game, Giraffe felt a sense of relief settling within him.

At the start of science class, the teacher tells everyone, ''Take out your books, and turn to page 254.''

She went on to lecture about friction and gravity. She explained that gravity is a force that pulls objects toward each other. ''This is why we all stay on the ground and why objects fall down when we drop them,'' she said.

The teacher then explained that friction is a force that opposes the motion of two surfaces that are touching. "This is why you might slip on a smooth surface and why it is easier to walk on a rough surface," she continued.

She gave some examples of gravity and friction in action to explain the concept further, "For example," she said, "gravity pulls the moon toward the Earth and friction keeps the moon from falling into the Earth."

Upon hearing these facts, Giraffe dove into his imagination. He started seeing himself jumping from one planet to another. As he was jumping to his third planet, he slipped because it was round so he couldn't keep his balance and slipped into the dark abyss of space. He shook his head to escape the vision.

He thought that if the planets were square or rectangle he would have landed on the planet better and been able to maintain his balance

At this time, he thought of a question, "Why are the planets not square?"

The teacher looked up from her teaching, and repeated, "Why are planets not square?"

She gave him a disgusted look, perplexed at his question.

Giraffe, not realizing he had spoken out loud tried to appease his teacher, "Why are planets round and not a different kind of shape like rectangle or square, pentagon, or hexagon?

The teacher's momentary confusion was quickly replaced with a composed demeanor, as she attempted to guide the conversation back to the lesson at hand. "Giraffe, your imagination is truly out of this world. Let's focus on the solar system for now," she said, trying to steer the conversation back to the lesson.

As the classroom filled with awkward silence, Eric leaned in, trying to lighten the mood. "Come on, Giraffe, your brain's orbiting a little too far out today. Let's keep it down to Earth for now," he teased, a twinkle of laughter in his eyes.

Giraffe shifted in his seat, feeling a wave of discomfort wash over him. The feeling of being out of place swept over him again, he was always not quite fitting into the conventional classroom. Despite the attempts to lighten the mood, he found it difficult to join in the laughter, the sting of being misunderstood lingering at the back of his mind.

Giraffe had mixed feelings, and he did not know what to say. He felt an odd one out, and embarrassed, but his curiosity did not let him relax. As the class went on, Giraffe couldn't stop thinking about the cool things in space. He felt determined to share his different ideas, even if they weren't in the book.

When he got home he was sad and went upstairs to his room. The question about "Why are planets round and not a different shape" was bothering him.. So he decided to go to his computer and search the internet for the question. After a few searches he found the answer:

> *Planets are round because of gravity. Gravity is a force that pulls all objects towards each other. The more massive an object is, the stronger its gravity is. Planets are very massive, so their gravity is very strong. This strong gravity pulls all of the material in a planet towards its center, forming a sphere.*

> *The only reason why planets are not perfectly spherical is because they are spinning. As a planet spins, its centrifugal force pushes the material on its equator outward. This makes the planet bulge at the equator and flatten at the poles. The faster a planet spins, the more pronounced this bulge will be (spaceplace.nasa.gov).*

He felt happy he had unlocked the answer to the question. He called his best friend, Chip Kelly, to come over and play some games. Chip lives a couple of houses away, so he arrived quickly. After they played Blox for a while, Giraffe asked Chip, "Do you know what happened today at school?"

Chip replied, "No, tell me what happened?"

Giraffe replied, "When I asked why are planets round, the teacher didn't know the answer but instead got mad at me, made fun of me, and the entire class started to laugh at me. I was so embarrassed that I wanted to jump out of the window."

Chip said, "Oh no, that's so sad."

Giraffe replied, "Yes, it is very sad. The question was in my mind so I decided to search Google for the answer and you know what? I found the answer!"

Chip jumped in excitement and said, "What? You found the answer?" He danced around the room repeating, "You found the answer! The teacher didn't know."

Giraffe shouted with excitement, "YES, I found the answer and learned the reason why planets are round."

18

Chip said with a devilish look in his eye," So, technically you are smarter than the teacher because you know something the teacher doesn't!"

Giraffe said calmly and ever-so-slightly, puffing his chest out, "I will tell the teacher tomorrow," then giggled.

Next day, Giraffe was very excited to share his discovery about the new found knowledge. When he got to school, he told his English teacher, "I know why planets are round!" His teacher was very kind and supportive. She said, "Great, that is a good thing to know," and encouraged him to share it with his science teacher.

Giraffe bounded toward his science class feeling good because his English teacher supported him. He decided to share why planets are round with his science teacher.

As the science teacher came into the class, he blurted out excitedly, "Planets are round because of gravity!" His teacher took a step back, from her impassioned student and said, "Well, of course they are, Mr. Smarty Pants. Are you trying to trick me and think you're smarter than I am?"

Then Giraffe said, "I may not be smarter than you but I found the answer to the question which was bothering me."

She was Infuriated when she heard this. She shouted at him,"You disrupt my class with your silliness, go sit down and get ready for class."

Giraffe felt very sad, and decided not to share anything with the science teacher ever again.

He felt like the lowest of the low, and decided he needed to make it seem like he was one of the newer students to hopefully change her attitude of him. He thought it was working, but realized the teachers grew frustrated by his behavior and his depression came back in full force. Giraffe knew that the more he tried to hide, the worse things got. When he did speak, he felt like his words were falling on deaf ears, which was incredibly frustrating. He felt like he was talking to a brick wall, and it was no use. Then Giraffe tried relieving his anger, and frustration issues by focusing on why he should be happy. Nothing worked. He walked through his day quiet and frustrated, with no escape from it. His mom, sensing something was troubling Giraffe asked, "Son, why do you look upset?"

Giraffe replied, "Mama, I don't want to go to school. School is bad."

Giraffe's mom replied, "I know you do not like school but sometimes you have to adjust yourself according to the environment."

Giraffe said, "Mama, I tried but nobody understands me there. Even teachers think I am bad. My classmates think I am dumb."

Mama told Giraffe, "I know you feel so helpless, especially when you are dealing with teachers but let me tell you that when you feel powerless, just believe that these times are there to teach you something. These struggles are going to make you stronger."

"But Mama," Giraffe said, "these struggles are not making me any stronger, in fact I am feeling weaker and more frustrated. I am losing my self-confidence. I do not want to go to school. You know it is bad for my mental health."

Giraffe's Mom replied, "If you know yourself then no one can ruin your mental health. Never let anyone dim your light. You are a star. I know you, and I believe that you will shine even in the darkest place."

CHAPTER THREE
DISAPPOINTMENT

Giraffe had never been a fan of school. To him, it felt like an endless cycle of wasted time and mundane lessons. Every morning, without fail, he would fall into a daily argument with his mom about why he should not have to go to school.

As the time to return to school approached once again, the intensity of their arguments began to rise. Giraffe voiced his frustrations, "Mama, I do not want to go to school. School is not time efficient, they spend hours explaining simple concepts. The lessons can be learned in just 10 minutes."

His mother, ever patient, responded, "Well, my dear, some people have short-term memory, and they need to hear things repeatedly to remember. It's better for them to reinforce their knowledge. And for those with sharp memory, repetition can help solidify their understanding."

Giraffe wasn't done yet. "But Mama, I really can't stand the emphasis on tests. It's like they measure our worth solely based on how well we perform on exams. But you know what? Scoring high on tests doesn't always mean you understand the concepts. Some students are just good at passing exams, not at grasping the real essence of what they're learning."

With determination, Giraffe pointed out, "I believe there are better ways to learn. I can explore the same concepts in a much more engaging way through internet platforms. There, I can delve into topics that truly pique my interest, and I can do it at my own pace, in-depth, without having to rely on teachers who might not even have a deep understanding of what they're supposed to be teaching us."

Giraffe thought about this, most of the time he felt quite frustrated when the teachers could not satisfy his questions. He seemed to have better knowledge than the teacher but teachers expected him to follow their way. This would always kill his imagination and creativity.

Giraffe's memory of a recent English creative writing project still lingered in his mind. It had been a source of excitement for both him and his mother, as they had poured their hearts into crafting a story with profound depth.

The writing prompt had been simple yet intriguing: continue the story of finding a mystery treasure in a jungle. However, Giraffe had dared to dream bigger. He had envisioned the greatest treasure imaginable in the universe, something beyond material wealth or jewels. For him, the most significant treasure was to find happiness and when he thought about finding happiness, he believed that helping others brings the ultimate happiness. So, he created the story that two friends went into a jungle to seek treasure. They searched for the treasure for so long but could not find any, so they decided to return home. On the way back, they saw that a tiny kitten had fallen in a dried well. When these boys saw the kitten in the well, they helped that kitten to come out of the well. They gave them something to eat and drink as well. Both the boys realized that the happiness achieved by helping others is the real treasure in the world.

When he reached home, he excitedly shared his perspective with his mother, she had been overjoyed and proud. She recognized the depth and profoundness of his thoughts, and her heart swelled with pride. She assured him, "Son, your thoughts are incredibly deep and insightful. You've made me so proud today. I have no doubt that you'll receive the highest marks for your exceptional creativity and perspective."

* * * * *

When the test results were finally handed back, Giraffe's excitement turned into confusion and sadness. Instead of the high marks he had anticipated, he received disappointing results. His teacher had given him unfavorable remarks for not providing more detailed descriptions and explanations in his story. She seemed unable to grasp the greatness of his concept and the depth of his beliefs.

Giraffe couldn't understand how his project, which he had poured his heart and soul into, had not been received as he had expected. It left him feeling bewildered and disheartened, wondering why his profound ideas had not been recognized and appreciated as he thought they would be.

After school, Giraffe was very depressed. Even during dinner, he remained unusually quiet. His mother immediately sensed that something was troubling him. With genuine concern, she gently asked Giraffe, "Is there something on your mind, my dear?"

Giraffe, with a heavy heart, finally opened up, "Mom, I received very low marks on my English Creative Writing project. You told me that I had made you proud, but in reality, I barely passed, and the teacher was not pleased with my work."

His mother's heart sank, filled with empathy, she approached him and enveloped him in a warm, reassuring hug. She spoke with unwavering love and wisdom, "My dear son, please don't let the teacher's words or the marks on a paper define your worth. Someone's inability to recognize your true value does not diminish your worthiness. Your thought process and creativity extend far beyond their comprehension. You should never feel disheartened. You have always made me immensely proud, and this grade doesn't change that."

Giraffe felt a surge of comfort and relief as his mother's words soothed him. He returned her loving embrace and whispered, "Thank you, Mom, for always knowing how to lift my spirits."

In that moment, Giraffe realized the profound depth of his mother's love and understanding, which provided solace and strength during times of doubt and disappointment.

Next day he did not want to go to school but as usual, after a long argument with his mom, he reluctantly went.

When he reached the school, he went to his friends and shared that he did not get good marks on the English test and he felt bad about how the teacher did not understand his message. He told them that his mom told him that his story is very deep and he lost marks because his teacher was not able to understand his intellectual level. However, instead of offering support or understanding, his friends responded with laughter and mockery.

"Haha, you think you're smarter than the teacher?" they teased. "In reality you are so dumb. Getting a C+. You suck. You can never be smarter than the teacher."

Embarrassed and hurt, Giraffe quickly clarified, "No, I didn't mean I'm smarter than the teacher. I meant that the teacher didn't understand the message I was trying to convey through the story."

Later, during the English period, his teacher discussed why some students had lost marks on the project. Giraffe couldn't help but inquire about his own performance and the reasons behind his lower score. The teacher, with a hint of frustration, explained, "Your storyline was very illogical. In your story, they did not find any treasure, whereas you needed to write a story where they discovered some treasure.

Giraffe replied, with conviction, that they did find the treasure of happiness.

The teacher, resolute in her stance, insisted that the concept of "treasure" in the context of the project meant a chest of gold or precious stones, something that could bring material wealth. She urged Giraffe to write about that type of treasure and refrain from using metaphors like "Happiness" or anything else.

After the class, the teacher asked Giraffe to stay behind, her voice gentle but firm. "You should concentrate on your studies, Giraffe. Your other interests seem to be taking up too much of your attention. Stick to the main points and answer the questions the way we've discussed in class."

Giraffe hesitated before responding, "But, teacher, I always want to share more information."

The teacher sighed, "Those extra details aren't always necessary. For example, in the English project, you aimed for creativity but missed the main idea."

Giraffe's confusion deepened, and a tinge of sadness settled in his heart. He couldn't fathom how to align his thoughts to please the teacher and get good grades.

The events at school had taken a toll on Giraffe's spirits, leaving him deeply upset. When he returned home, his mother, concerned for her son, asked him about his day. Holding back tears, Giraffe shared the entire distressing episode with his mother.

Giraffe felt the burden of the day's events weighing him down, draining the usual sparkle from his eyes and leaving him adrift in a fog of uncertainty. With each passing day, his grades suffered, a stark reflection of his inner turmoil. The more he tried to study hard, the worse his grades got. Teachers and students avoided him so much he started to feel like a ghost.

With final exams looming closer, the principal took the initiative to call Giraffe's parents, recognizing the need for a collaborative effort to support and guide Giraffe through this challenging phase of his academic journey.

The following day, Giraffe's mother visited the principal's office, where both the teacher and the principal were present. The principal began by expressing his concerns, "Giraffe does not seem to be focusing well on his studies and that is why his grades suffer. Is there something going on at home that could be affecting his performance?

Giraffe's mom, in response, spoke warmly about her son, "Giraffe is ambitious and a bright kid." She continued by highlighting his intelligence and his tendency to see things from a unique perspective. She acknowledged, that Giraffe sometimes struggled to articulate his thoughts effectively, leading to a feeling of being out of place and causing him stress.

The teacher then chimed in, "It was crucial for Giraffe to learn how to answer questions in line with the established teaching approach. I am afraid he will continue to achieve poor grades if he persists in answering questions his own way."

The principal advised, "As a parent, you should encourage Giraffe to study diligently and adhere to the teachings in class rather than relying solely on his own research on internet platforms."

Giraffe's mother accepted the advice with hesitation. She was aware that Giraffe learned more quickly and effectively through the internet platforms he liked to use. She recognized the core issue: the teachers attempted to confine Giraffe's thinking within the education system's traditional framework. This led to Giraffe's frustration, as he couldn't fully unleash his potential.

Later that evening, after dinner, Giraffe's mother approached him. "Giraffe, I know you're a brilliant kid, but to excel in your exams, you need to adhere to a certain structure."

Already overwhelmed by frustration, his mother's words left him feeling utterly helpless. He longed to escape his young life, yearning for a way out that seemed elusive. In his mind, he began envisioning an escape to the Amazon, to discover true essence beyond the restrictions he faced.

CHAPTER FOUR

PLANNING
THE ADVENTURE

Giraffe was disheartened by the warning he received from the principal.

He tried to study hard. Despite his hard work he was not able to improve his grades. He felt invisible at school. No one seemed to understand him.

He kept thinking about the school and the education system and how severely it sucked. Several times teachers would ask students to create assignments about the things, which he didn't think useful in daily life or would have any use in future. Giraffe always wanted to experience life to the fullest. He wanted to learn how to survive in nature, how to experience different parts of the world, what is life and what is soul? He had countless questions in his mind about how life was created, how we get thoughts in our head, but whenever he asks these questions, people around him make fun of him. Only his mom encouraged him to talk about such things, but even she had not been able to satisfy his questions.

While returning from school, he noticed his senior classmates were gathered around a small kitten. The fluffy creature captured his attention with its undeniable cuteness, prompting Giraffe to approach the group and join in their playful revelry. Little did he know that this innocent decision would unravel a sequence of events that would forever leave a mark on his young heart.

As Giraffe neared the gathering, his initial excitement gave way to a chilling realization. To his horror, he discovered that these older boys were not engaging in friendly play with the defenseless kitten; instead, they were subjecting the tiny creature to cruel blows with a stick. His heart sank, and he couldn't help but cry out in despair, "Stop! It's just a small kitten! Don't hurt it!"

The senior boys responded with mischievous laughter, mocking his compassion. "Look at little Giraffe trying to be a hero," they taunted, their laughter echoing around the scene.

One of the boys, fueled by a disturbing idea, proposed, "Let's teach this Giraffe what we're teaching this kitten," and the others eagerly agreed. With cruel intent, they turned their attention from the helpless kitten to Giraffe himself, raising their sticks menacingly.

Emotions swirled within Giraffe as he faced this unexpected turn of events. Embarrassment, confusion, and pain gnawed at his young soul. In a desperate bid to escape the impending torment, he turned and fled as fast as his trembling legs would carry him. But even as he distanced himself from the tormentors, an overwhelming sense of sadness enveloped him. He forgot to rescue the kitten, and a deep sense of helplessness lingered, knowing the older boys' strength and size had made him powerless at that moment.

Upon returning home, Giraffe's somber mood did not go unnoticed by his mother. With maternal intuition, she sensed that something was amiss and gently inquired, "What happened, Giraffe?"?"

He started crying, his mom hugged him tightly. He told her what happened when he tried to save the kitten.

His mother, her heart aching for her distraught son, listened attentively to his tale. After he had shared every detail of the distressing encounter, she began to speak with a wisdom born of compassion and experience.

"Son, I understand your pain," she said, her voice a soothing balm to his wounded spirit. "You did a brave and honorable thing by standing up against cruelty, even when you felt so small and insignificant."

Pausing for a moment to let her words sink in, she continued, "There will be moments in life when we face situations where we seem powerless in the face of authority. But always remember, that true strength lies in holding onto your morals and values, refusing to be swayed by those who are on the wrong path."

With a gentle, reassuring smile, she imparted her most profound wisdom, "I know it's not easy to stand against them, my dear, so you'll need strength. And the best way to find that strength is to remember God is always by your side. When God stands with you, no force in the universe can harm you. Because God made everything and controls everything."

Curiosity sparkled in Giraffe's eyes as he asked, "Mama, how can we have the ancient beings by our side?"

She replied with unwavering faith, "Through prayer, my love. When you pray from the depths of your heart, the ancient beings hear you and answer. They can give you the strength to stand tall, even against the most formidable of authorities."

As the words of his mother washed over him, Giraffe felt a newfound sense of ease and empowerment. He understood that, with the divine presence guiding him, he could navigate the challenges of life with unwavering courage and grace.

The day had been a particularly challenging one at school. Giraffe had reached a breaking point, and he needed an escape from the suffocating routine that had become his daily life. Giraffe and Chip Kelly were hanging out as usual, sharing their griefs about school.

As they shared their thoughts, Chip's eyes lit up with a mischievous glint. "Let's go and explore the world on our own," he proposed with an air of excitement. "We can learn on the internet and live life the way we want to."

Giraffe's heart leaped at the suggestion. His eyes sparkled with newfound hope and enthusiasm. "Yes," he exclaimed, "let's do this!"

But soon a shadow of doubt crept over Giraffe. "Our parents would never allow us to go alone," he admitted, his voice tinged with uncertainty. "How would we ever convince them?"

Chip Kelly, always the quick thinker, furrowed his brow in thought. He had an ace up his sleeve, an idea that would turn their dreams into reality. "I've got it!" he exclaimed, his eyes dancing with mischief. "My uncle, Mr. John, is the coolest person I know. He's wise, fun, and he lives just a stone's throw away from the Amazon Jungle."

Giraffe's curiosity was piqued. "What's so special about Mr. John?" he inquired.

Chip grinned, his eyes alight with nostalgia. "Every summer, I look forward to visiting him. We do the most amazing things together. He lets me wander in the wilds, even late at night. He reads the most incredible stories to me and shares his adventurous tales. Mr. John is incredibly knowledge-able, and guess what? He's explored the Amazon Rainforest himself. He knows the fun and benefits of adventures like no one else."

With a wide smile, Chip Kelly continued, "I'm going to visit him again this summer, and you should come along. I'm sure he'll allow us to explore the Amazon with him."

Giraffe's heart swelled with happiness. He could hardly contain his excitement. "That sounds like a plan," he declared, a newfound sense of purpose filling his being. "I can't wait for summer vacation!"

As the sun dipped below the horizon, casting long shadows across the porch, Giraffe and Chip Kelly felt a sense of hope and anticipation. The world was vast and full of wonders, and they were about to embark on an adventure of a lifetime, guided by the wisdom and boundless spirit of Mr. John.

Giraffe, with an eager gleam in his eyes, approached his mom for permission, "Mom, can Chip Kelly and I go visit his Uncle John in the Amazon? His stories are so incredible, he is very wise and most importantly he lives very close to the Amazon. He is adventurous and he knows the Amazon very well, and we're dying to explore the wonders of the rainforest!"

Giraffe's Mom's brow furrowed with concern, responded gently, "Oh, my dear, the Amazon

Rainforest can be quite wild and unpredictable. I worry it might not be safe for you two to go alone."

Chip Kelly chimed in, his voice brimming with enthusiasm, "But we'll be really careful! We've been studying all about the rainforest, and we'll follow every precaution. We won't take any unnecessary risks."

Giraffe nodded fervently, adding, "Absolutely! Chip's Uncle John will guide us every step of the way. He's like a walking encyclopedia about the Amazon!" Giraffe continued, "Mom, the Amazon boasts some of the oldest trees in the world. Can you imagine the stories they hold, each one a witness to centuries of life and history?"

Chip Kelly's enthusiasm echoed, "And the rivers, they're like magical pathways. The Amazon River is the heartbeat of the rainforest, teaming with life! We might even spot those pink river dolphins that we read about!"

Giraffe picked up where Chip ended, and added more reasons why they should be allowed to go, "And the legend of El Dorado! Mom, imagine stepping into the same lands that explorers have ventured into for centuries, all in pursuit of a city of gold. It's like living out an adventure tale!"

Chip Kelly added with a grin, "Exactly! Even if we don't find El Dorado, just being in the Amazon, surrounded by its mysteries and wonders, would be the greatest adventure of our lives! Please, let Giraffe come, it's a chance of a lifetime!"

With a hopeful glint in his eye, Giraffe made a final plea, "Please, Mom, it's a once-in-a-lifetime opportunity! We'll learn so much about the rainforest, its incredible creatures, and the magic of nature. And we promise to share every exciting detail with you when we're back!"

Chip Kelly added with a grin, "Yeah, and we'll take tons of pictures! It'll be like we're living in a real-life adventure book!"

Giraffe's Mom, trying to balance caution with understanding, explained, "I understand your excitement, but it's crucial to think about your safety. Let's take some time to carefully consider all the aspects." She stared hard at the two boys resisting the urge of jumping up and down in front of her as she thought. They were so excited, how could she not allow them to go, "Alright, boys, if you really want to go to the Amazon, you need to have a solid plan. Start by researching more about the place. Make a list of things you'll need for your trip."

Giraffe said excitedly, "Sure, Mom! We'll do it right away. We'll find out everything about the Amazon, from the dangerous animals to the tricky spots we need to watch out for."

Chip Kelly said, "We'll watch tons of videos and read all the websites we can find. We'll be experts on the Amazon by the time we're done!"

Giraffe's Mom felt happy to see their enthusiasm, "That sounds like a solid plan, boys. Just make sure you're thorough and stay safe. Adventure is great, but safety always comes first."

Giraffe and Chip Kelly started their research with enthusiasm, as they wanted to impress his mom that they had enough knowledge about the Amazon rainforest. They sat hunched over Giraffe's laptop, their eyes glued to the screen as they watched an array of videos and read articles, gathering valuable insights about the Amazon jungle.

Giraffe leaned back, rubbing his eyes. "There's so much to learn about the Amazon. Did you know it's the largest rainforest in the world?"

Chip Kelly nodded eagerly, his fingers flying over the keyboard. "Yeah, and check this out, Giraffe!

These AI programs can simulate the sounds of the jungle. We can use them to familiarize ourselves with what we might hear out there."

Giraffe's eyes widened in fascination. "That's amazing! And look at this video. It's showing us how to identify different types of animal tracks. This will definitely come in handy."

Chip Kelly grinned, pointing at the screen. "And these satellite images on this map platform give us a detailed view of the jungle's terrain. We can plan our route more effectively with this information."

The more they delved into the wonders of the Amazon through their research, the more their anticipation and eagerness to explore the Amazon increased.

Giraffe nodded, impressed by their research progress. "You're right, Chip Kelly, with all this knowledge at our fingertips, we'll be more than ready to take on the Amazon rainforest."

One day they were researching the Amazon and found some astonishing facts.

Giraffe said, "Hey Chip Kelly, did you know that some trees in the Amazon Rainforest are incredibly ancient? There's a baobab tree that's believed to be over 6,000 years old!"

Chip Kelly replied, "Wow, that's mind-boggling, Giraffe! And speaking of ancient trees, have you heard about the Great Basin bristlecone pine, Methuselah? It's more than 4,800 years old, making it one of the oldest living organisms on Earth!"

Giraffe: "That's incredible, Chip Kelly, I did not know that."

Together, they dedicated countless hours to their research, their shared enthusiasm propelling them forward into the captivating depths of the jungle's mysteries.

They started making notes of all their research to keep the facts handy. They researched about the dangers to expect in the wild. They asked AI platforms to tell them what to expect in the Amazon Jungle. They found out that the Amazon is home to a wide variety of wild animals, some of which can be dangerous. These include snakes, spiders, jaguars, caimans, and piranhas. There are a large number of insects, some of which can be venomous. These include mosquitoes, which can transmit diseases such as malaria and yellow fever, and bullet ants, whose sting is said to be the most painful in the world.

Giraffe said, "Okay, Chip Kelly, we need to be prepared for anything in the Amazon Jungle. What do you think we should bring to keep us safe from the animals and other creatures?"

Chip Kelly replied in agreement, "Definitely, Giraffe. How about some strong rope? We can use it to set up barriers or make traps if we encounter any dangerous creatures."

Giraffe said, "That's a good idea. We should also pack some pepper spray. It might help deter any aggressive animals if they get too close."

Chip Kelly replied, "Right. And what about a loud whistle? If we find ourselves in trouble, we can use it to scare off animals and attract attention."

Giraffe said, "Excellent. We'll also need a reliable knife. It could come in handy for protection or even cutting through thick vegetation."

Chip Kelly: "Agreed. And let's not forget a sturdy, lightweight net. It could serve as an extra layer of defense if we come across any unexpected threats."

Giraffe: "Perfect. We'll be well-equipped to handle whatever challenges come our way in the jungle."

Since Giraffe often went camping in the wild with his parents, he had all the camping equipment.

They also decided they would need a first aid kit with medicine, and band aids. Giraffe insisted on keeping a dozen bottles of mosquito repellent; he did not want to get malaria. He stuffed his backpack with all the supplies to keep everything together.

When they were ready, they eagerly presented their findings to Giraffe's parents, their backpacks brimming with carefully curated supplies essential for survival in the Amazon. They also enthusiastically shared their comprehensive knowledge of the rainforest's wonders and perils to Giraffe's parents.

As he delved into the depths of his newfound purpose, something quite extraordinary occurred, his grades in school began to get even better. It felt like discovering the key to his passion didn't just unlock a door to happiness but it created a positive impact on all aspects of life.

Giraffe's mother was glad to see how much research the boys did. It really became their pastime to research more and more about the Amazon. She saw they enjoyed learning what they might encounter on their trip so much that they could spend hours on the computer without being bored or getting tired.

Giraffe's mother beamed with pride, acknowledging their thorough preparation. "Your dedication to planning for your Amazon trip is truly commendable," she remarked, casting a glance at Giraffe's equally impressed father.

Her sentiments were echoed by Giraffe's father, who nodded approvingly, "You've both shown incredible initiative and responsibility. I have no doubt that you'll navigate the Amazon Jungle admirably. You have our blessing to spend your summer vacation with Chip's Uncle John."

Giraffe and Chip's spirits soared. They were really going to spend their summer vacation with Uncle John in the Amazon Rainforest!

Giraffe impatiently waited for summer vacation. He counted every day and the minutes to see them pass.

As the days did pass and summer vacation drew nearer, Chip continued to amuse Giraffe with stories about his uncle's adventures. One day, as they sat beneath the shade of a tall oak tree, Chip offered a word of caution.

"Giraffe," he began, his tone serious, "you need to be prepared for something astonishing. In the heart of the Amazon, we might encounter people from different tribes who have had no contact with the outer world. It's a world unlike anything you've ever seen."

Giraffe, his eyes widening with wonder, asked, "How can there be people who've never had contact with the outer world? Are you saying they don't even have Wi-Fi?"

The absurdity of the idea struck them both, and laughter bubbled up from within. They chuckled heartily as they pondered the notion of life without Wi-Fi.

Giraffe, still chuckling, remarked, "I can't even imagine it! If there's no Wi-Fi, there's no reason to live."

Their shared laughter echoed through the tranquil afternoon, a testament to the modern world's dependence on technology.

CHAPTER FIVE

BEGINNING THE ADVENTURE

At last, the first day of summer vacation arrived; Giraffe and Chip's excitement skyrocketed. Early in the morning, Giraffe rose from bed, had his breakfast, got dressed, and grabbed his backpack with essential supplies that he had been adding to for several weeks. Giraffe had always dreamed of going to the Amazon rainforest, and it was finally here! He could barely contain himself, as his parents embraced him tightly. His mother offered him some last-minute advice before they were to set out on their grand adventure.

"The Amazon rainforest is a beautiful and fascinating place, but it can also be dangerous. So, always be prepared to meet unexpected dangers." She continued, "When you feel the danger, always trust your instincts. You could find yourself too close to dangerous animals, such as lions, snakes, or even venomous plants. Wild animals might be angry and hungry, so try to avoid these situations. And remember that love is always the best solution. Always! Treat others with kindness. You may not get the reward immediately, but it will eventually come."

* * * * *

Giraffe and Chip were scheduled to board a flight. At the airport, their parents bid them farewell. The two friends anticipated the adventure that awaited them with bright eyes. Although they had journeyed extensively with their parents, this marked their first solo travel experience, and they were glad to be going together.

After a long trip, they at last were welcomed by the sight of Uncle John, a wise old goat with a rugged-yet-amiable demeanor. His warm embrace enveloped the two young adventurers, instantly making them feel at home in the heart of the jungle. Uncle John's eyes twinkled with delight. "Giraffe, Chip, welcome to my humble abode. I trust the journey was not too arduous?"

Giraffe and Chip entered the house and settled into plush sofas in Uncle John's lounge. The boys found themselves surrounded by a captivating assortment of historical artifacts from across the world. Each piece seemed to carry a tale of Uncle John's remarkable adventures, narrating the rich story of his travels and explorations.

Giraffe's gaze roamed over an intricately carved totem from the depths of the Amazon, while Chip's eyes were drawn to a weathered map, its edges frayed with age, evoking tales of long-lost voyages and uncharted territories. The air in the room hummed with a sense of history and mystery, inviting the young explorers to embark on a journey through time and space with every artifact that adorned the walls.

"So, how was the trip here?" Uncle John asked again, as Giraffe and Chip Kelly exchanged a sheepish grin, momentarily startled by Uncle John's voice that brought them back from their reverie. Eager to engage in conversation, Chip responded, "It was incredible."

Giraffe said, "No, Uncle John, the journey was nothing compared to the excitement of being here with you!"

Chip nodded vigorously, his hair flipping and flopping with every movement. "Yeah, Uncle John, we can't wait to explore everything you've been telling us about. The stories we have learned about the creatures and the hidden treasures have us completely intrigued."

Uncle John chuckled, a rumbling sound that seemed to echo through the night. "Ah, the Amazon has a way of capturing one's imagination, doesn't it? But remember, my young adventurers, the jungle is both friend and foe. You must learn to respect its ways and listen to its secrets if you wish to uncover its true wonders."

Giraffe's eyes widened with wonder as they fixated on the remarkable collection before him. He couldn't help but gravitate towards a particular figurine, its intricate details fascinated him. But before he could utter a question, Uncle John preemptively shared the story behind the artifact.

"This, my dear Giraffe, is the La Tolita figurine," Uncle John began, his voice laced with the weight of history. "It's one among a series of exquisite ceramic figurines crafted by the La Tolita culture, a vibrant civilization that thrived in the heart of the Amazon rainforest from 400 BC to 600 AD. Note the intricate headdress, the meticulous facial features, and the stylized body that shows the rich heritage of the region. I stumbled upon it during an expedition in the Amazon five years ago."

Uncle John continued, "These figures hold a sacred significance, carrying the ancestral wisdom of the ancient beings within them. Their primary duty is to safeguard the city and its innocent inhabitants. They come to life when the city or its people confront life-threatening dangers."

Chip Kelly's eyes shimmered with fascination as they locked onto an intricate golden raft artifact. Observing Chip Kelly's captivated gaze, Uncle John leaned in to share the intriguing history behind the remarkable piece. "Ah, this is a part of the famed Muisca Raft," he began, his voice carrying a weight of reverence for the ancient treasure.

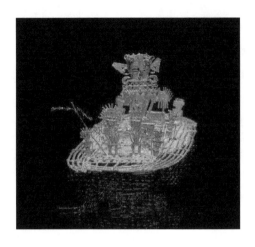

"Crafted from pure gold, this raft is one of the most celebrated works of Muisca art. I came across it during an expedition to the heart of the Amazon," Uncle John explained. "It is believed to depict the sacred initiation ceremony of a new ruler, an invaluable testament to the rich cultural heritage of the region."

Giraffe's eyes widened in awe at the sight of the magnificent Raft of Musica, a captivating artifact that left an indelible impression on his young mind. Turning to Uncle John with a mixture of curiosity and excitement, he asked, "Uncle John, do you think the legendary city of Gold, El Dorado, still exists?"

A spark of enthusiasm ignited in Uncle John's eyes as he responded, "My dear, while many deem it a mere myth, I am convinced that El Dorado is more than just a legend. I firmly believe that the city is waiting to be discovered, and mark my words, one day, I will unveil its ancient mysteries."

The shared fervor between Giraffe, Chip Kelly, and Uncle John was palpable as they nodded in unison. "Yes, together we will uncover the secrets of El Dorado," they affirmed, their hearts set on the goal of unveiling the enigma of the mythical city of gold.

Uncle John retrieved an aged map tucked away in a dusty corner of the room, gently placing it upon the table. With eager anticipation, both young explorers gathered around the table, their wide eyes fixated on the mysterious document. Uncle John carefully unrolled the ancient map, revealing its weathered edges and signs of age.

Pointing at a small 'X' marked along the winding course of the Amazon River, Uncle John pointed to a spot that held the promise of El Dorado. "Do you see this marking?" he inquired. "This may well be the location of the fabled city. This map, I found on one of my expeditions, is the oldest known map of the Amazon, and it's the only map with the presumed whereabouts of El Dorado."

Giraffe and Chip's excitement soared to new heights, and in unison, they eagerly asked, "Uncle John, when can we embark on our journey to the Amazon?"

With a smile, Uncle John responded, "My dears, you've had a long journey. Rest for today, and we shall set out for the Amazon tomorrow morning."

Throughout the evening, Uncle John shared his stories of adventures. With each anecdote and revelation, he painted a vivid portrait of the Amazon, illuminating its hidden dangers, its intrinsic beauty, and the delicate balance that defines its very existence.

Enthralled by the depth of his understanding, the two young adventurers found themselves drawn into a world beyond their wildest imaginations, where every shadow held a secret and every rustle in the underbrush whispered of ancient mysteries. Uncle John's profound insights and genuine passion for the Amazon filled their heads with even more anticipation for the adventure at hand.

CHAPTER SIX

THE ADVENTURE

As the morning came, and they anxiously waited for Uncle John to wake up, Giraffe suddenly realized that in the excitement of finally getting to Uncle John's home, he didn't know where his backpack was. Frantically, he began searching, but Giraffe noticed the grin on Chip's face and soon found out it was a prank. "Haha I had the bag the whole time, it's right here!" said Chip, quietly, of course, because Uncle John was still sleeping. Chip shrugged his shoulders as Giraffe shot him an angry snarl, but then sighed in relief to have recovered his backpack. "I had to find something to pass the time," Chip offered.

Giraffe responded "Not funny, Chip, you scared me so much."

* * * * *

When Uncle John finally awoke, they prepared their things and quickly left for their adventure. Although Uncle John insisted on making breakfast, Giraffe and Chip could barely eat the tiniest bit of food–they just wanted to leave. All three of them got into Uncle John's Jeep and traveled into the deep jungle of the Amazon. The journey was a mesmerizing trip through a tapestry of landscapes, cultures, and ecosystems.

As they drove farther into the jungle, the air felt a lot heavier with moisture, the sounds got softer, and the scenery more serene. Soon, they found themselves navigating winding roads that snaked through rolling hills and verdant valleys. The movement made them feel a little dizzy, so they stopped to walk around a little until the feeling subsided. Realizing they had been traveling a few hours already, they started to get hungry, so they found some delicious berries, superb guava and acacia leaves. They absolutely savoured the berries and acacia leaves.

They drove even farther, as ancient trees loomed overhead, their massive roots intertwining and creating an intricate tapestry of life. As night fell, they decided to sleep and dreamed of all they had seen so far on their adventure.

When they awoke the next morning, they immediately headed out to search for El Dorado. Rivers emerged, their waters shimmering under the dappled sunlight filtering through the thick canopy. They embarked next on a boat, its motor humming softly as they glided along the water's surface. When the boat finally came to a stop, they found they needed to continue on foot, so they started walking, before too long, they came upon a lion.

Uncle John screamed, "AHHHH a lion, run!" The lion roared, and showed its large teeth, then charged at them, but while Chip and Uncle John were screaming at the top of their lungs, Giraffe was brave and didn't run or scream. Instead, he stood strong in front of the beast and asked, "Why do you look so worried?"

The lion replied, quite breathlessly, "I'm looking for my baby. A tribe tried to kidnap us, so I had to flee. In the pursuit, they hit me on my head–I must have lost consciousness. When I came to, my baby was gone. They took him. I must find my baby!"

Giraffe replied, "I'm sorry you had to go through that, I can't imagine how hard it must have been for you to lose your baby, but do not worry, we can help you find your baby." Chip Kelly added, "We have long necks to get an aerial view and find him from afar."

Next Uncle John asked, "Why did they take your son?"

The Lion replied, "They are looking for El Dorado. It is a lost ancient city of gold and they believe that it can be found only by pleasing the ancient beings, who once sent wrath on the people of Musica and buried the entire city when they refused to offer them gold."

All three of them got excited when they heard of El Dorado, but felt bad for the lion. They had a lot of questions and had a hard time not all asking at once.

Chip asked, "What do you know about El Dorado? How can we find the city?"

Uncle John inquired, "You think they took your son to please the ancient beings to find El Dorado?"

Giraffe said, "How can we help you find your son?"

The great beast peered at them, head cocked inquisitively and said, "You are full of questions, it seems you are also in search of El Dorado. If I help you, will you help me find my son?"

Uncle John replied "Correct, we are in search of El Dorado and many different artifacts."

Giraffe added, "I came to the Amazon to learn how to survive in the wild and experience learning in a fun way; I knew I would learn much more about life and different things by experiencing it here instead of learning in a boring and useless way in school. But now I just want to help you find your son."

Lion smiled and said, "You sound a lot like my son, little one; he also hates school. Now let me tell you what I know about El Dorado. I am sure you know that El Dorado was buried by the ancient ones, when they got angry at Musica people. Now, the wolf tribe wants to take over the Amazon and rule the rainforest. They are searching for gold to gain more power. They believe that the ancient ones can only be pleased with the sacrifice of a pure soul. My son seems to be the best candidate for this sacrificial ritual because he is very innocent and very kind. He is always willing to help people without any expectations of any type of reward, which makes him a pure soul."

Uncle John replied, "They are right that they need to please the ancient beings by the pure souls but not by sacrificing the pure soul, instead they need to please them by becoming the pure soul through loving people and being kind to them. Kindness and love will please them. Sacrificing a pure soul will make them angrier than before."

Uncle John further added, "My research shows that the ancient ones only love those who have pure souls and show themselves to only those who are pure souls."

Chip asked, "What is a pure soul? How can someone get one?"

Uncle John replied, "A pure soul is someone who is filled with love. Their soul is not polluted by worries, hatred, or fear."

Lion agreed with Uncle John.

Giraffe said, "Let's search for your baby and rescue him. Which direction do you think they went when they took him?"

With this, the four adventurers together began their search for the cub.

CHAPTER SEVEN

THE ESCAPE

Lion introduced himself as Leo, the guardian of the jungle, he explained as they walked that his elders passed down knowledge through generations. Leo had heard whispers of El Dorado (as all lions do). They all asked lion questions and found they were forming a trust and bond as they continued. They liked Leo, and were enthralled with his stories. Leo recognized Uncle John's connection to the land. Leo confirmed Uncle John's research and findings, as he talked about hidden landmarks, natural wonders, and the sacred river that carved a path through the heart of the jungle.

Determined to save the cub and thwart the wicked plans of the wolf tribe, Giraffe, Chip, Uncle John and Lion persisted in their search for Lion's son, and discussed a plan to infiltrate the tribe's hidden temple.

They went through treacherous terrain on foot where they encountered venomous creatures, navigated harrowing river currents, and braved the mysterious depths of the jungle.

As their journey deeper into the jungle continued, Giraffe and Chip marveled at the ancient trees that towered majestically overhead. Uncle John pointed out the trees and said, "Look at these trees, they are more than a thousand years old, they could tell tales of centuries long past."

Chip's curiosity arose as he listened intently to Uncle John's explanation. "But how can you tell their age, Uncle John?" he inquired, his eyes alight with fascination.

Uncle John smiled as he replied, "My dear Chip, these trees hold within them the secrets of time. Each scar, each hollow, tells a tale of the countless seasons they have weathered. The scars from lightning strikes and fires, the marks of human encounters, and the hollowed trunks that provide sanctuary to the forest's creatures all bear witness to the passage of centuries. It is through these profound signs etched upon their ancient bark that we come to understand their age and life."

As Giraffe and Chip trudged through the thick Amazon jungle, the trees and bushes seemed to meld into an impenetrable wall of green. They couldn't tell which way was which anymore, and the sunlight barely managed to peek through the thick leaves above, casting eerie shadows on the forest floor.

Uncle John unfolded the aged map he had shown Giraffe and Chip back at the house, to check their route. The map confirmed Leo's guidance, and showed they were getting closer to where the old city of El Dorado was rumored to be. As they neared the edge of the mighty Amazon river they saw the receded water unveiled stone face and carvings etched into the riverbed.

Leo pointed out that the faces, nearly 2000 years old, were the handiwork of the ancient Musica people. They were created to guide the people of the city to the hidden passages leading to their treasure troves in the subterranean gold mines.

Giraffe shouted as he pointed at one stone that showed what looked like a tower with ancient writing, "Hey, look what I found! There's some kind of ancient writing on this stone. Do you think it's a clue?"

Uncle John said, "Let me take a closer look. This inscription speaks of an old legend, a tale of a temple hidden deep within the jungle." Uncle John's eyes fixed on the stone with profound intensity as he voiced, "This seems to be directing us toward the temple. We better hurry. This could be where the Evil Wolf tribe might perform the sacrificial ceremony."

Leo, his brows furrowed in concern: "Be cautious, my friends. The Evil Wolf tribe is not to be underestimated, but we must save my boy."

Chip, his eyes wide with as much excitement as fear, "Whoa, this is like an adventure straight out of my favorite books! We're really going to find a hidden temple? This is going to be so awesome! But are we really going to have to fight the Evil Wolf tribe?"

With Leo and Uncle John as their guides, they looked down the path leading to the tribe's hidden temple, and they all felt the danger intensify. The path was surely guarded by traps and watchful eyes.

Leo realizing this said, "Considering there likely will be an even heavier guard presence at the temple entrance, we need a careful strategy if we're to be successful."

The group put their heads together and came up with a quick plan.

Uncle John suggested, "We'll set up nets tied between the trees near the entrance." Motioning to Chip, he continued, "You can call out to grab their attention. Once the guards approach, we can pull the nets swiftly and trap them, suspending them from the ground." He then turned to Giraffe and handed him a small spray bottle, "Once the guards are ensnared, you can spray them with this mixture derived from the curare and jimson weed herbs of the Amazon. It will make them fall unconscious."

Giraffe shook his head in agreement, eyes wide with nervousness.

Leo nodded in approval, "Alright, then let's execute the plan. We'll lay the nets in strategic positions, ensuring we trap them all." He handed out the three large nets from Giraffe's backpack and they all quietly went about placing them in the three locations they had discussed.

Suddenly, Chip let out a shrill cry. The sound pierced through the dense silence of the jungle, making all the guards jump, and look around for its source. Hidden under the cover of trees, Leo, Giraffe, and Uncle John waited in intense anticipation.

The guards inched toward where they thought the sound had come from, unaware of the trap that awaited them. As they approached, the net suddenly sprung up, capturing them in its tight mesh. Giraffe then leaped forward as planned, and sprayed the liquid at the guards and they instantly fell asleep.

Leo's Race to Save His Son

They carefully opened the gate and entered the temple. Leo thought it best for Uncle John, Giraffe and Chip to remain at the temple entrance and await his return while he ventured inside to search for his son. The lion shared that his knowledge of the ancient temple's layout, gleaned from his own youthful explorations, would guide him through the maze of corridors and hidden chambers.

The temple was a place of power and mystery, its walls were adorned with cryptic symbols and the halls seemed to pulsate with otherworldly energy. The air was heavy with the smell of incense as Leo, the regal lion, padded silently through the dimly lit temple. His senses were on high alert as he sought out his son.

As he approached the chamber where he could feel his son was held captive, Leo could hear what he presumed were other temple guards talking in distant murmurs that traveled in hushed sounds through the stone passageways. He knew he had to act quickly and discreetly. His cub's life depended on it.

He retrieved a dart with poisoned tip that he always carried with him, and launched it silently towards the unsuspecting guards. As the dart struck its mark, the guard collapsed instantly. Retrieving darts again and again, one by one, Leo neutralized the guards, clearing his path to his cub. The cage was secured with tough vine ropes, specially crafted from thick Amazonian vines. Using another tool, a knife from his special carry sack, Leo sliced through the vines to liberate his cub.

At last the cub was free, and Leo and his son shared an emotional embrace, "I thought I had lost you." Leo whispered to his cub. They then exchanged a determined look, silently acknowledging the challenges that still lay ahead. Their journey was far from complete; in fact, it was about to become even more treacherous as they faced the daunting task of navigating through the temple.

Leo raced through the temple's corridors, his son in his arms, and the guards hot on his heels. He dodged their clumsy attempts to capture him, his knowledge of the temple's layout giving him a clear advantage. They twisted and turned, turned and twisted, until they finally found themselves back at the temple entrance, where Uncle John, Giraffe and Chip waited nervously.

The group, reunited, spared not a moment for celebration, and instead raced into the jungle together. The familiar jungle offered them a sense of refuge this time, even though the temple's imposing facade loomed behind them, a symbol of the challenges they had faced.

The Wolf Tribe and the guards not far behind, they had to steel themselves for what lay ahead.

CHAPTER EIGHT

THE FINAL FIGHT

As they neared a clearing of the jungle, they found the Wolf Tribe standing in front of them waiting to attack and capture the cub to sacrifice him; before they could retreat and head back toward the temple, they saw more of the Wolf Tribe racing at them. Turning back toward the clearing, Evil Wolf, their leader, stepped forward with a long sword raised over his head.

Evil Wolf gave a deep howl and shouted at them, "You can't defeat Wolves, we will find the Gold and get all the power to rule the world." He gestured the sword toward Leo, "Hand over your son to me. His life needs to be sacrificed to please the ancient ones of Musica."

Leo, his cub, Uncle John, Giraffe and Chip all froze. Then Giraffe, a wise and kind soul, stepped forward to challenge the Wolf's distorted logic. With a calm and steady voice, Giraffe voiced a truth that cut through the sinister air they encountered in the clearing of the jungle.

Giraffe said, "You can't please the ancients by hurting others. Do you think El Dorado would be yours even if your sacrifice would be accepted? The ancient ones know you intend to use power and money for evil purposes. The ancient beings will never favor evil."

A glint of frustration moved across Evil Wolf's smile. Giraffe's words struck a chord that resonated beyond the immediate threat, exposing the hollowness of the pack's plans. The notion of using a sacrifice to attain power was not only morally reprehensible, but it also stood in contrast to the true nature of the jungle – a delicate balance where life and death coexisted in harmony. Giraffe wasn't sure if the Wolves could see the error in their judgement, but they were definitely confused by a youngster standing up to them with such conviction.

Evil Wolf's growl echoed through the jungle at the challenge to his dominance. But Leo, cub, and Giraffe now stood united against the darkness that sought to envelope them.

As the tension in the air escalated. They needed a plan, a strategy that would give them a fighting chance against the odds stacked against them. Uncle John glanced around, evaluating their surroundings. The jungle's dense vegetation offered both cover and potential obstacles that could be used to their advantage. Uncle John and Leo shared a knowing glance then immediately took action.

With a quick but subtle gesture, Leo signalled to his son to stay close. Uncle John guided Chip Kelly and Giraffe to take the opposite side of Leo to create a distraction to the Wolf Tribe. They slowly moved to a position where they could better leverage the terrain.

Their first move was to use the jungle's cover to their advantage. Uncle John shouted, "Hide!" And the boys, Leo, and Uncle John ducked behind trees and undergrowth, they scattered, and weaved their way through the dense trees to create confusion among the Wolves. The Evil Wolf's growls filled the air as he commanded his pack to encircle them, but Leo's swift movements and Uncle John's knowledge of the jungle allowed them to remain one step ahead.

Then, Leo and Giraffe unleashed a series of distraction tactics. They mimicked the calls of other animals they had learned about in their extensive research, creating the illusion of multiple sources of noise to confuse the wolves. They threw rocks to different locations, causing the Wolves to turn their attention away from their precise location.

As chaos erupted among the Wolves, Leo seized the opportunity to take down a couple of Wolves, utilizing his darts with the precision of a seasoned hunter. His moves were calculated and efficient, a testament to years of surviving in the unforgiving jungle.

However, the Evil Wolf was not to be underestimated. With a roar, he rallied his remaining tribe, determined to capture the cub at all costs. Leo knew that they had to keep moving, to stay ahead of their pursuers. Wolf finally got hold of the cub. His tribe captured Leo, Chip and Uncle John.

As Giraffe, hidden among the dense foliage, observed the distressing scene unfold, his heart sank. He realized that the situation had taken a dire turn. Determination burned in his eyes as he vowed to himself that he wouldn't let his friends down, but at the same time his heart felt extremely heavy with helplessness. His mother's words echoed in his mind like a beacon of hope, "If you are on the right path against stronger evil, you are never alone. God is always with you." The memory of her guidance brought him comfort in this dire situation.

He felt hot tears start to form at the corners of his eyes as he prayed with all of his heart, "I call on the ancient beings who protect this jungle, to please give me strength to save my friends." In that moment of vulnerability and surrender, Giraffe felt a deep connection with something greater than himself. A profound sense of calm washed over him, and he could almost sense the presence of an invisible force, or forces, a feeling of a guiding light that reassured him he was not alone in this battle.

Giraffe stood in awe as a radiant figure appeared before him, emanating an otherworldly aura of pure white light. Giraffe recognized the figure immediately as it was the same figure which he saw in Uncle John's collection of artifacts.

The ancient one addressed him, "Giraffe, you have a pure heart filled with love and kindness. You asked for strength to save your friends." He gave him a big diamond necklace and told him, "Take this amulet. It is precious and powerful. When you wear this amulet, you will become invincible. It will shield you against every evil and make you immensely powerful so no one can stand against you."

Giraffe looked up at the ancient god-like figure covered by a white light, his gratitude shining in his eyes. "Thank you," he whispered, his voice filled with humility and determination. He placed the necklace around Giraffe's neck, feeling its cool touch against his skin. Instantly, he sensed a change within him – a heightened awareness, an indomitable spirit, and a newfound courage that transcended his physical form. He knew that this necklace was more than just a beautiful treasure; it was a symbol of the unwavering love, kindness, and faith that had brought him to this moment.

The ancient being smiled gently, a warm reassurance that made Giraffe feel like he was being hugged by the whole universe. With a nod, the being began to ascend back into the sky, leaving behind a sense of serenity and empowerment that lingered in the air.

In the heart of the jungle, Giraffe stood alone. His heart pounded in his chest, as he clasped the necklace around his neck. All at once, a brilliant light burst from the necklace. It was as if he had captured a piece of the sun itself. The light expanded, encircling him, forming a protective shield that shimmered like a bubble.

The shield radiated an intense heat, a force so powerful nothing could penetrate it. Giraffe could feel the energy pulsating around him, a warm, comforting presence tha filled him with courage.

Giraffe marched forward confidently piercing through the Wolf Tribe. The presence radiated with an aura of invincibility, his determination fortified by the purity of his heart and the divine amulet.

The Wolf Tribe advanced toward Giraffe as Uncle John, Leo, Chip, and even the Evil Wolf, who was still holding the cub, all stared in astonishment. The Wolf Tribe attacked with all their might, their weapons clashing against the light shield, but instead turned the weapons to sparks and flames the second they touched it. The shield stood strong, its light burning brighter with every strike.

Wave after wave came toward the light shield, but none could penetrate it. The Wolf Tribe lay confused, and shaking on the ground.

Before Evil Wolf could make a run for it with cub, or place a final attack to try to steal the power, Giraffe turned his power toward Evil Wolf. With a final surge of power, Giraffe pushed a radiant burst of light over the clearing, engulfing it completely. The evil ones fell to the ground instantly, and the good guys were spared. Cub ran to his father as Leo scooped him up into his arms once again.

CHAPTER NINE
FINDING EL DORADO

Leo's heart swelled with relief and joy as he finally reunited with his son. They ran into each other's arms and gave the biggest, tightest hug ever. Then they all heard a loud crack that shook the jungle floor.

Within minutes, a phantom city emerged from beneath the ground where the loud crack had split the ground. The city that had been hidden for centuries, purely made of gold. The houses, the buildings, all of the structures – all shined with the rich, warm hue of precious metal. It was as if the very earth had transformed into a treasure trove.

Amidst the golden landscape, precious gemstones sparkled like stars in the daylight. Rubies, emeralds, sapphires, and diamonds adorned the city like vibrant ornaments. Some were implanted in the walls of the structures, while others hung from trees, catching the sunlight and casting colorful rainbows and reflections across the surroundings.

Everyone was awe-struck at the sight. Uncle John leapt and hooted as the city came into view after years of searching for it without resolution–at last, El Dorado had been found! Giraffe, too, was overwhelmed with happiness. To witness a city materialize from the ground, made of gold, was undoubtedly a dream. He rubbed his eyes to make sure he wasn't in fact dreaming.

Evil Wolf was utterly astounded by what he saw before him. His eyes widened in disbelief; this was the city that could give him the power to rule the entire world! Despite the breathtaking beauty of the city, his villainous thoughts continued to race through his mind. While everyone was busy praising the beautiful city, he slowly moved toward Giraffe knowing that he could not take over the city without a sacrifice.

Evil Wolf sweetly approached Giraffe in a facade of friendliness, then took out a sharp dagger and lurched toward Giraffe. "Give me that necklace!" he growled.

But just as the wolf came close to Giraffe, and the dagger make contact with the shield, the necklace glowed again, and a bright light burst out of it. The light was so strong that it struck Evil Wolf and pushed him away, away with a loud "Whoosh!" and he sent tumbling into a nearby chasm that resembled a deep well. He plummeted, disappearing from sight and never to be seen again.

After defeating Evil Wolf and his Wolf Tribe, Giraffe gingerly removed the glimmering necklace. The protective shield dissipated, and the light returned inside the necklace. Giraffe was happy to save the cub and his friend from Evil Wolf. He stood dizzy after wearing the necklace, and seeing the marvels of the ancient lost city.

Leo, the cub, Uncle John, Chip and Giraffe all came together and celebrated before they explored El Dorado.

Chip jumped from place to place, his eyes wide with wonder as he discovered every detail of the golden city. Uncle John's excitement bubbled as he delved deeper into the mysteries of the newly discovered ancient city, pouring over every artifact, inscription, and symbol. With a camera in hand and a keen eye, he eagerly snapped pictures and collected items that would fuel further study and exploration.

Leo and his cub walked hand-in-hand, talking and pointing at the structures and statues that told the story of its glorious past. And Giraffe, the hero of the day, just stood there, his eyes reflecting the golden glow of the city. He seemed to be soaking up all the wisdom and power of the ancient beings.

Finally, Leo and his cub approached Giraffe, their eyes shone a blend of gratitude and relief. In a deeply heartfelt gesture, Leo embraced Giraffe, his powerful frame conveying emotions that words couldn't capture.

"Dear Giraffe," Leo began, his voice resonating with sincerity, "you are a young lad, full of energy, with a heart pure and brimming with kindness and compassion. I cannot thank you enough for saving my son."

Giraffe, taken aback by Leo's heartfelt words, could only smile in response. He had done what any friend would do, yet Leo's gratitude made him feel like he had saved the world. Leo and his cub, then said goodbye to their new friends, and left to go home.

As the golden hues of the sunset painted the sky, the trio of adventurers made their way back to Uncle John's home. Each step carried a sense of happiness and pride, the accomplishment of unraveling the secrets hidden within the heart of the ancient city adding a new chapter to their shared journey.

CHAPTER TEN
THE RETURN

The weary trio, Uncle John, Giraffe, and Chip, finally reached the familiar comfort of Uncle John's home. The fatigue from their adventure clung to their bones, but the warmth of their cozy home embraced them.

The morning brought with it a new energy. The boys were excited to share their journey with their parents. They spoke of the ancient city's marvels, the newfound companionship with Leo and his cub, and the uncharted territories they explored. In response. Their parents, beaming with pride, listened to their child's courageous account, feeling a surge of joy at the remarkable achievements.

Uncle John called the Department of Archaeology and informed them about the discovery of the ancient city–hoping they would protect it. The news spread like a wildfire. Several news agencies started contacting Uncle John and soon the great trio of adventurers became famous and they were on all news channels.

The phone continued to ring, filled with congratulations, interview requests, and messages from friends and well-wishers. The once-ordinary trio found themselves swept up in a whirlwind, their lives forever changed by the ancient secrets they unearthed in the heart of the Amazon.

As Summer vacation came to a close, Giraffe and Chip prepared to return home. Over dinner, they found themselves immersed in the memories of their exhilarating adventure and the discovery of the ancient city.

Giraffe reflected on how a mere desire to visit the Amazon turned into a remarkable discovery. Chip added, "Indeed, we had to put in the effort to prove that we were worthy of such an adventure."

Uncle John, wise and understanding, nodded in agreement. "The world is a strange place, and people are even weirder. Everyone has their own way of looking at the world, and the way they look at the world shapes their future reality."

Curious, Chip leaned forward and asked, "What do you mean, Uncle John?"

Uncle John smiled, his eyes filled with the wisdom of a lifetime. "You see, I always believed that El Dorado existed in this world, and I wanted to see it with my own eyes. and now I have."

He shifted his gaze toward Giraffe, who seemed lost in contemplation, and addressed him with a knowing smile, "Giraffe, my dear, your insatiable curiosity led you to seek experiences beyond the confines of a classroom. You always yearned to unveil the mysteries of the Amazon Jungle, to learn the essence of survival in its heart. And now, here you stand, having lived through one of the most extraordinary adventures, experiencing life in a way that no school could ever teach."

Gazing at Chip, the one who sought joy and adventure in every nook and cranny, he chuckled and said, "And you, Chip, are curious in your own right, but a great friend who is always on the lookout for a good time and an adventure to spice things up. I'm sure this journey provided you with ample adventure, didn't it?"

Giraffe broke the silence, his voice filled with a sense of wonder, "This adventure has taught us more than we could ever learn in school."

Chip nodded in agreement, "We may not have solved complex mathematical equations, but we learned how to survive in the jungle. And who would have thought that our simple intention to save a small cub would lead us to uncover a city that had been hidden from the world for centuries?"

Uncle John leaned in and said, "School should teach you about the wonders of the world, the beauty of exploration, and the importance of curiosity. They should teach you how to think NOT what to think. But, more often than not, it falls short, when they end up judging the students by grades and the performance in tests or exams.

Uncle John further added, "Look at you, despite your below-average academic performance, you excelled when given the opportunity to channel your curiosity in the right direction, unraveling some of the greatest mysteries of the world. The main dilemma lies in the fact that children are becoming smarter and more curious at a faster rate than their teachers can keep up with. The traditional teaching methods that worked 400 years ago are no longer sufficient. It's time for the education system to evolve."

Uncle John leaned back in his chair and summarized, "Boys, you achieve what you want in life, but you need to believe that you can achieve it. Always remember, people will never understand your dreams and passions. They will criticize you and try to stop you from going after your dreams, because they can never believe that they can achieve any dreams. They cast their reality onto you. Do not make their faulty vision of life your reality. Otherwise, you will never be able to achieve your dream."

The two adventurers listened intently, absorbing the profound wisdom that Uncle John had shared.

The next day, Giraffe and Chip returned home, where they received a warm welcome from their parents and friends who were eagerly waiting to hear the stories from the adventurers.

The school year soon began, and as Giraffe stepped onto the school premises, a crowd gathered around him. He felt a sense of celebrity. His class fellows and students from other classes wanted to find out the details of his adventure.

The school principal approached Giraffe. At first he wasn't sure what the principal might say, but he was relieved when he put his arm around Giraffe saying, "Giraffe, I must say, your accomplishment has left me utterly astonished. It's a true testament to the notion that greatness is within reach for anyone who believes in themselves and follows their dreams. I am genuinely proud of you."

Giraffe responded, "Thank you, Principal. I appreciate your kind words."

Principal further added, "I want to acknowledge something too, Giraffe. Our traditional education system fails to recognize the unique talents of students like you. It's a flaw in the system. But you, with your courage and determination, proved that pursuing one's dreams can lead to incredible achievements. Not everyone has that kind of courage."

Giraffe nodded, "It wasn't easy, but I'm glad I took the leap. Education should inspire curiosity and creativity."

Principal agreed, "Absolutely, Giraffe. In fact, I believe your experience holds valuable lessons for us. It's time to rethink our approach to education. Would you be interested in contributing to the redesign of our education system?

Giraffe happily agreed, "That would be amazing! I would love to help make learning more enjoyable for everyone."

Principal said, "Excellent! Let's embark on this new journey together. Your insight will undoubtedly play a pivotal role in shaping the future of education in our school."

Impressed by Giraffe's insights, the principal appointed Giraffe as an advisor to contribute to the redesign of the education system. A new journey began, and Giraffe's dream of transforming the education system appeared to be on the verge of becoming a reality. The school embarked on a path of innovation and improvement under Giraffe's guidance.

ABOUT THE AUTHOR

Zoraib Nadeem, a young author, is not only passionate about writing but also vocal about creating positive changes in his community. With a strong focus on revolutionizing the global education system, he is determined to make a meaningful impact. Alongside his academic brilliance at a young age, he enjoys the intellectual challenges of playing chess, showcasing his strategic thinking, and problem-solving skills.

Made in the USA
Middletown, DE
01 November 2024

63160685R00057